JAN CARR
The Nature of the Beast

PICTURES BY
G. BRIAN KARAS

TAMBOURINE BOOKS   NEW YORK

Ketchup

Dad's red (only) ties

Beast
by Isabelle

Text copyright © 1996 by Jan Carr

Illustrations copyright © 1996 by G. Brian Karas

Printed in the United States of America. The text type is Bodoni.

The illustrations were created using acrylic, gouache, and pencil.

Library of Congress Cataloging in Publication Data

Carr, Jan. The nature of the beast / by Jan Carr ; illustrated by G. Brian Karas.

p. cm. Summary: When Isabelle buys a beast on special at the pet store, her father thinks it will be

an interesting scientific experiment, but her mother says it will have to go if it continues its loud

imitations of her French lessons. [1. Pets—Fiction.] I. Karas, G. Brian, ill. II. Title.

PZ7.C22947Nat 1996 [E]—dc20 95-40675 CIP AC

ISBN 0-688-13596-X (tr.)—ISBN 0-688-13597-8 (lib. bdg.)

10 9 8 7 6 5 4 3 2 1

First edition

For Charlie,
whose sweet, quirky little nature
I love to observe — *J.C.*

To Oliver — *G.B.K.*

One morning I was wishing for a friend. Instead, I found a crisp dollar bill face up on the sidewalk.

"Can I keep it?" I asked.

"Buy whatever you want," said Dad.

"As long as it's something quiet," Mom agreed.

So I walked into town and went straight to the pet store.
Dogs were too expensive, and so were cats. I didn't want a fish,
and I didn't want a gerbil. But there happened to be a special
on beasts.

The salesman told me everything I needed to know. "You'll know when Beast is happy," he said. "He'll chant, chirp, and chatter."

When I got home, I snuck Beast in through the back door. Dad was bent over one of his experiments. Mom was preparing a French class for her students. As we tiptoed past, she dropped her pencil.

"*C'est la vie,*" she shrugged.

Suddenly Beast started to rasp and rumble. His voice came out deep and gravelly.

"SAAAAY LA VEEEEE!" he bellowed.

Mom dropped her notebook too.

"Please can I keep him?" I begged.

"No," Mom declared.

Dad rubbed his chin. "A creature that speaks," he said. "Actually, that could be very interesting. From a scientific standpoint—Of course! That's it!"

Dad grabbed one of Mom's notebooks. He wrote something
across the front cover. THE NATURE OF THE BEAST, it said. He
handed the notebook to me.

"Isabelle," he instructed, "your job is to watch the beast carefully and write down everything he does. What he likes, what he doesn't, how he behaves—"

"Beast speaks," I wrote.

"There's my little scientist!" Dad ruffled my hair.

Mom, however, did not look pleased. "If he makes too much noise," she warned, "back to the store Beast goes!"

In the days that followed, I found out a lot of things about Beast. I watched him sleep. I wrote, "Likes to nap in the chandelier."

I watched him clean himself. I wrote, "Spits on paw ten times exactly, then lathers up his fur."

I watched him raid Dad's closet. I wrote, "Likes red ties only."

Dad was happy (mostly) with the way the experiment was
going. Mom still wasn't sure.

"SAAAAY LA VEEEEE!" Beast rumbled.

"I love you, Beast," I whispered in his ear. Beast was funny
and furry.

Each day, I watched my big, woolly friend. Each day, I learned more about him.

"Dances to the drone of the dishwasher," I wrote.

"Likes ketchup. Moos for more."

"Howls to the ring of the phone."

"AHOOOOOOOOOOOOH!"

"Too much racket!" shrieked Mom.

Uh oh!

The next morning, Mom got on the phone with the pet store. "We'd like to bring Beast back," I heard her tell the clerk. "Today."

"No!" I cried. "Not my Beast!"

But when I ran to find him, I noticed something different.

"Slept *under* the chandelier," I wrote.

"Spit on paw one time only. Forgot to groom his fur."

"Cried at the click of the phone."

I ran to Dad.

"I think Beast is sick," I said.

"No tricks," Mom interrupted. "My mind's made up. He's going back."

Just then, Beast wobbled into the room. His voice was
weak and quavering. "Say la vee," he whimpered.

"He *is* sick!" cried Mom.

We rushed Beast to the vet.

The vet peered in Beast's ears. She looked in his mouth and tapped on his stomach. She stuck a thermometer under his tongue.

I was worried. Dad was worried. Mom looked worried too!

"Your beast is very sick," the vet told us. "You got him here just in time!"

When we got home, I set up a bed for Beast. Mom gave Beast his medicine. Dad came in with a plaque. TO ISABELLE, it said, OUR YOUNG SCIENTIST. SHE SAVED BEAST'S LIFE USING SCIENTIFIC OBSERVATION.

"Does this mean Beast can stay?" I asked.

Beast let out a tiny whimper.

"Poor Beast," cooed Mom. I could tell Mom liked Beast
fine as long as he was quiet.

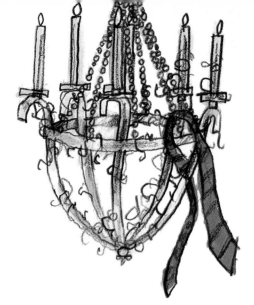

After a few days in bed, though, Beast was back to his beastly ways.

"Where are all my red ties?" shouted Dad.

"We just *cleaned* that chandelier!" cried Mom.

"SAAAAAY LA VEEEEE!" boomed Beast.

That was it. Mom clapped Beast up by the ruff of his neck.

Oh, no! I was afraid Beast had really botched things now.

But Mom didn't yell, and she didn't throw Beast out. All she did was open up her French book.

"Beast," she said firmly, "If you're going to tromp all around the house shouting out in French, I have only one thing to say to you. You've *got* to learn some new words!"

Beast leapt up to the chandelier. "BON JOOOOOOUR!" he tried, swinging this way and that.

"Beast is happy," I wrote.

So was I.